I Wish I'd Been Born
A Unicorn

'I Wish I'd Been Born a Unicorn'
An original concept by Rachel Lyon
© Rachel Lyon

Illustrated by Andrea Ringli

Published by MAVERICK ARTS PUBLISHING LTD

Studio 3A, City Business Centre, 6 Brighton Road,

Horsham, West Sussex, RH13 5BB

© Maverick Arts Publishing Limited February 2016

+44 (0)1403 256941

A CIP catalogue record for this book is available at the British Library.

ISBN 978-1-84886-196-1

www.maverickbooks.co.uk

This book is rated as: Green Band (Guided Reading)
The original picture book text for this story has been modified
by the author to be an early reader.

I Wish I'd Been Born
A Unicorn

by Rachel Lyon
illustrated by Andrea Ringli

Mucky was a smelly horse.

He liked to roll in mud.

The other horses would not
play with him.

They said he was too dirty
and had fleas.

"I wish I'd been born
a unicorn," said Mucky.

"Then I would have friends."

"I can make your wish come true,"
said a clever Owl.

"You'll see."

Owl went to the cows and asked for some cream.

"I want to help Mucky," he said.

The cows gave him some cream.

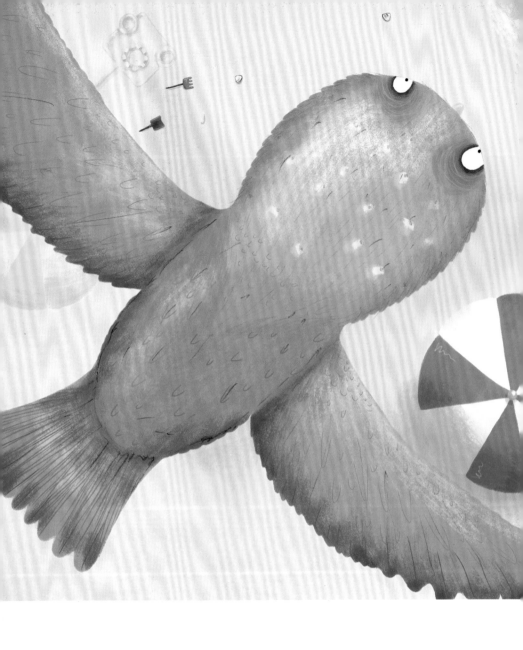

Then Owl went to the beach
to find a pointy shell.

Owl painted Mucky with the cream
and tied the pointy shell on his head.

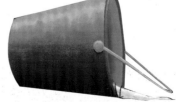

In the morning, the cows

got a surprise.

"That's not Mucky!" they said.

"It's a unicorn!"

Mucky was very happy. "It's true!"
he said. "I am a unicorn!"

Suddenly Owl saw a dark cloud
and began to worry.

It started to rain hard.

The rain washed the cream away.

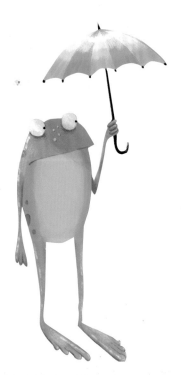

Everyone felt sad for Mucky.

"We will make more cream,"
the cows said. "Please don't cry."

Mucky smiled. "Do you really care about me?" he asked. "Yes," they said.

"Then I do have friends!" Mucky said.

"I'm glad I'm not a unicorn after all.
You like me just the way I am."

Quiz

1. What does Mucky like to do?
a) Roll in mud
b) Go on a picnic
c) Go to the seaside

2. What does the owl use to turn Mucky white?
a) Mud
b) Paint
c) Cream

3. Where does the owl go to find a shell for Mucky's horn?
a) The beach
b) The mountain
c) The shop

4. What happens to turn Mucky from a unicorn back into a horse?
a) He licks off the cream
b) He has a bath
c) It rains

5. Why is Mucky glad that he is not a unicorn?
a) Because he doesn't like to be clean
b) Because his friends like him just as he is.
c) Because it is hard work

Turn over for answers

Maverick Early Readers

Our early readers have been adapted from the original picture books so that children can make the essential transition from listener to reader. All of these books have been book banded, for guided reading, to the industry standard and edited by a leading educational consultant.

Green Band

Yuck! Said the Yak Early Reader
ISBN 978-1-84886-176-3

I Wish I'd Been Born a Unicorn Early Reader
ISBN 978-1-84886-196-1

Orange Band

The Black and White Club Early Reader
ISBN 978-1-84886-179-4

Gold Star for George Early Reader
ISBN 978-1-84886-197-8

A Scarf and a Half Early Reader
ISBN 978-1-84886-177-0

Pirates Don't Drive Diggers Early Reader
ISBN 978-1-84886-195-4

Turquoise Band

Preposterous Rhinoceros Early Reader
ISBN 978-1-84886-180-0

Hocus Pocus Diplodocus Early Reader
ISBN 978-1-84886-178-7

Grumpy King Colin Early Reader
ISBN 978-1-84886-194-7

The Four Little Pigs Early Reader
ISBN 978-1-84886-193-0

Quiz Answers: 1a, 2c, 3a, 4c, 5b